By Sarah Tatler   Illustrated by Dale Gottlieb

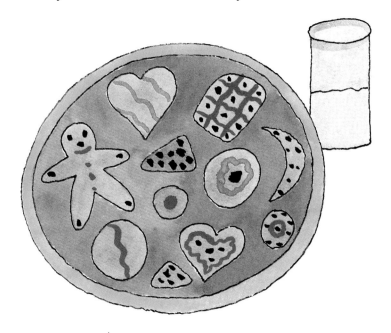

 ScottForesman

A Division of HarperCollins*Publishers*

Mix, mix, mixing.

Shape, shape, shaping.

Bake, bake, baking.

Sniff, sniff, sniffing.

Taste, taste, tasting.
Yum, yum, yummy!

Teaching People How to Treat Me

Val and Joan were chattering away about which girls liked which boys and whether or not the couples seemed suited for each other.

One couple they just couldn't figure out. "I don't know why Mary likes Tom so much," Val said. "Every time she says something, he cuts her down," she continued. "He says, 'So what?' to everything she says."

"Yeah! He really is rude to her," Joan agreed. "I wouldn't let a boy talk to me like that. I'd teach him how to treat me nicely, or I wouldn't be his girlfriend anymore."

Positive thought: I can teach people how to treat me nicely.

Peaceful Sleep

When Ms. Harris tucked her eight-year-old daughter, Darlene, into bed, she could see the worry lines creasing her little forehead.

"What's on your mind, honey?" her mom asked.

"Oh, I was just wondering, Mom. Wondering if I passed my math test. Wondering if I made the school play. Wondering if James will still be mad at me tomorrow," Darlene answered.

"Is there anything you can do about those things tonight?" Mom asked.

Darlene thought for a few minutes. You could almost see her considering each possibility.

"No, Mom, there's nothing I could do to get the answers tonight. But it's hard to rest with these thoughts running around in my mind," Darlene sighed.

"Let me give you a back rub," Mom offered. "See if that helps."

Mom rubbed Darlene's back, and the young girl began to feel safe and sound. As her body relaxed, so did her mind.

"Umm, thanks Mom," Darlene said dreamily as Mom tiptoed out of the room.

Positive thought: As my body relaxes, so does my mind.

Praying to Win

After months of hard work, Ken's basketball team had made it to the play-offs. He wanted to win the pennant more than anything else in the world. The evening before the final game, Ken talked with his dad about how important winning was to him.

"Dad," he said, "is it okay to pray that my team wins tomorrow? I really want to win, but I feel a little funny asking God to help me beat the other team."

"The reason you feel funny," his dad said, "is that deep inside you know that God is for everyone. It's certainly okay to pray about the game though. Why don't you pray that you play the best you can and that you enjoy the game no matter what the outcome?"

Positive thought: God is for all of us.

Less than Perfect

Today was "one of those days" for Ted. It started when he whispered to his friend Noah that he had a crush on a girl, and it came out loud enough for the whole class to hear. Ted turned the color of a tomato. Then he spent the rest of the day reliving the incident—just like instant replay on Monday night football. Each time he thought about it, he felt embarrassed all over again.

That night, Ted watched several TV shows to get his mind off things. One show was an old *I Love Lucy* rerun that his mom was watching. Lucy was working on the assembly line in a candy factory. But the conveyor belt full of candy was moving faster than Lucy's hands, and she got herself in a terrible, chocolatey mess.

On another show, a teenage girl got in trouble for cheating on a test at school. On still another, Ted found himself laughing at the troubles the father kept getting himself into.

Watching these programs, Ted realized that no one is perfect. TV shows were even centered around people's silly mistakes and their results.

Ted decided that if he did something stupid once in a while, he'd just learn to live with it—and to quit worrying about it.

Positive thought: I can live through my less than perfect days.

Old Movies

David and Melissa flopped down on the carpeted floor in the den, their eyes glued on the TV. Mom and Dad were in chairs nearby, also in rapt attention.

They were all watching *The Sound of Music*—for at least the fifth or sixth time. But no matter. They laughed harder than ever when Sister Maria blew the whistle at the rude, rich captain. And the children now knew all the lyrics to the songs, so they sang along enthusiastically.

And when a really fun scene was about to happen, the children elbowed each other, enjoying the anticipation, not just the event.

"It's nice to know that we don't always need something new and different," Mom said, petting their terrier Missy. "I'm glad we can enjoy some things over and over."

Positive thought: I can enjoy some things over and over.

The Stress Test

Mrs. Jones brought in an article to show her fourth-grade students. It was about how certain life events—like losing a job or the death of a loved one—cause a lot of stress for adults.

"If people have a number of these things happen at once," Mrs. Jones said, "you can almost predict that they will get sick. Lots of stress is often followed by illness.

"What events would you list that are very stressful for children?" Mrs. Jones asked.

Stephanie, sitting in the back row, didn't have to think twice about what had really been hard for her to handle: moving. And switching schools midyear.

Nearby, Seth felt his stomach crunch. "Divorce," he thought. "My parents' divorce still makes me feel sick."

Slowly, the students in Mrs. Jones's class began to raise their hands, and Mrs. Jones listed their stressful events on the chalkboard.

Looking over the list, Mrs. Jones said, "My goodness—we've got a list as long as the newspaper's. I guess it's not always easy being a kid, is it?"

Positive thought: The first step in handling the stress in my life is knowing I have it.

The Jigsaw Puzzle

Sheila was just itching to put together one of the two new jigsaw puzzles she had received for her birthday.

Should she do the red-and-blue striped balloons first? Or the three grey kittens in a basket? Deciding on the latter, Sheila got the card table out of the hall closet and set it up.

Then she dumped all the puzzle pieces on the table and started turning the colorful sides up.

Just then, Dad wandered in from a walk. Soon he had pulled up a chair and was busily matching colors to the photograph on the box.

Then Sheila's younger brother Desmond came in. "Can I help, sister?" he asked.

"Sure," said Sheila. "You try to find all the pieces that have a straight edge. I like to find those first—sort of like a frame for the picture."

When Mom came in the den later, she had to smile at the sight of her family hunched over the game, busily working and chatting together.

"Who would have thought a simple puzzle could keep so many people happy?" she said, laughing and shaking her head.

Positive thought: Playing with my family brings us closer together.

The Scared Turkey

Brad ran into the cabin, yelling. "Dad," he said, breathless. "You won't believe what just happened to me."

"What, son?" Dad asked, putting down his novel.

"I was walking down the hollow and came across a wild turkey. He was clucking and screeching something fierce. I was trying to ease away, so I wouldn't disturb him, but he saw me."

"Uh-oh," Dad said. A cornered wild turkey could be bad news.

"He went crazy, Dad. I guess he was scared of me, so he turned and started running. But the only thing behind him was the fence surrounding the pigs. So he just ran into that—again, and again. That turkey just kept butting into that fence, falling back, and trying again. I thought he was going to kill himself trying to get away."

"But *you* got away okay?" Dad asked.

"Yes, I slipped away and he took off flying. But it was amazing, Dad. In order to get away from something it was afraid of, that turkey blindly ran into something *much* more dangerous. And the funny thing was, I wasn't a threat at all."

Positive thought: Facing my fears is more productive than running from them.

I Make a Difference

"I want to give some money to help the homeless," Chan said to his older sister.

"You couldn't possibly give enough money to really help them," his sister replied. "What are you going to donate, a *dollar?*"

Mom was in earshot, and she spoke up. "I'm glad you want to donate some money," she said to Chan. "I know a social worker who works with a shelter in the city. I'll give you her number so you can call and find out where to send your gift."

Chan called and got the information. That afternoon he mailed a one-dollar bill wrapped in a piece of white paper to the shelter. A note was enclosed.

A few days later Chan received a letter in the mail. It was from St. Luke's Shelter. The note thanked him for his donation and told him that it would be used to make copies of coloring pages for the children who stayed there.

The end of the note read, "Thanks so much. People like you make a difference."

Positive thought: I make a difference.

Flower Power

M argaret was studying flowers in science class. Her head was full of thoughts of flower parts like pistils and stamens.

When her Grandpa Carlton and Grandma Nancy heard about this, they invited Margaret to go with them on their weekly wildflower hunt. This is how Margaret found herself at Black Rock Mountain, winding up a well-trodden trail. She breathed in the woodsy smell of moist leaves, bark, and rich soil.

At first, everything looked green or brown under the hazy light of the forest overhang. But soon she began to notice other colors. First, she spotted a brilliant red, spidery plant on a tall stem. She saw one, two, then dozens of them.

"Look, Grandma and Grandpa," she said.

"Yes, that's bee balm," Grandpa said. "Hummingbirds love it, and Indians used to use it to soothe insect bites."

"You know," Grandma added, "wildflowers travel. If we come back next year, there might not be any of these left in this spot. They'll have moved."

But Margaret's biggest find was three different colors of the same flower: rose, white, and purple trilliums. Together, she and her grandparents peered closely into a trillium's droopy shell, and Margaret saw the flower parts she and had seen and read about in her textbook.

"It's a miracle," she whispered to Grandma and Grandpa. "Why, the plants have a whole life of their own—traveling, making beautiful new flowers. It's something I never thought about before."

Positive thought: Miracles are happening all around me.

Other works by Anne D. Mather and Louise B. Weldon…

Around the Year with the Cat at the Door
Affirmation Activities for Ages Five and Older
> *by Anne D. Mather and Louise B. Weldon*
>
> *Around the Year with the Cat at the Door* provides 50 child-tested, hands-on lesson plans and activities that build and enhance self-esteem, problem-solving, and decision-making skills. These activities also help children explore values such as gratitude, honesty, and forgiveness. Twenty-five reproducible handouts are included. A wonderful teacher's guide for sharing feelings, beating boredom, and fishing for good thoughts. Workbook, 87 pp.

Order No. 1476

Cat Tales
A Place for Me to Write My Thoughts
> *by Anne D. Mather and Louise B. Weldon*
>
> Written especially for children, the positive thoughts found on each page of this journal capture the joys and successes of young children; nurture the development of a healthy sense of self; and provide children with a creative outlet for expressing their feelings, challenges, and dreams. Whether they choose to write or draw, children are provided with ample space to document their thoughts. 192 pp.

Order No. 8331

**For price and order information, or a free catalog,
please call our Telephone Representatives.**

HAZELDEN

1-800-328-0098	**1-612-257-4010**	**1-612-257-1331**
(Toll Free. U.S. and Canada, and the Virgin Islands)	(Outside the U.S. and Canada)	(24-Hour FAX)

Pleasant Valley Road • P.O. Box 176 • Center City, MN 55012-0176